ASL Tales:

RAPUNZEL

Written and Illustrated
by
Judy Hood

Created and Performed in American Sign Language
by
Pinky Aiello

ASL Tales Canada

ASL Tales Canada

The Publisher, Judy Hood, and Pinky Aiello would like to thank Joe Hood,
Bonnie Lund, Marcia Michel, Audrey Perino, Vincent Iubatti,
Jonas Hartley, the rest of the ASL Tales Team, and especially Fred Sawyer.

First Edition 2008

ISBN 978-0-9811486-0-1

14 13 12 11 10 09 · 8 7 6 5 4 3 2 1

Design by Janis Sawyer

ASL consultation by Alisha Bronk

Printed in Canada by Friesens

ASL Tales Canada
Calgary, Alberta

Visit us at ASLTales.net

Judy Hood, Author and Illustrator, would like to thank
Laurie Meyer, who has become a dear friend, the Deaf community, especially,
and Janis and Fred Sawyer
for their countless hours and tireless dedication to bring
this book to fruition.

To American Sign Language and the people who love it.

Laurie Meyer Co-Founder

ASL Tales

Once upon a time in a far away land,
a young man and his wife lived
beside a big stone wall.

On the other side of this
wall lived a Witch; a Witch
with a beautiful garden.

Every day the wife would peer out at the Witch's garden and the gigantic vegetables growing there. "I must have some," she said, "or I might die."

"I'll take my chances with the Witch," thought the husband.

That night he climbed the wall and brought back a basket of greens. His wife made them into a salad and ate them with glee.

The next day she demanded more and the next even more!

One dark night as the husband gathered his stolen vegetables, the Witch sprang out from behind a tree.

"You!"

"You dare to steal from me?" She smiled her witch smile. "If you give me your first born child, I'll let you go free."

The husband agreed. What else could he do?

The day came when the couple were blessed with a baby girl. No sooner had the babe come into the world than the Witch paid her a visit. She snatched the child and away she went. She called her

Rapunzel

Oh, how the Witch loved Rapunzel.
She showered her with gifts:

kittens
and
chocolate
and
dolls

Everything was fine until the day of Rapunzel's twelfth birthday, and then the Witch took her to a tower and locked her...

inside.

7

Rapunzel was mystified.
She was *horrified*.
She was *frightened.*
She stamped her feet.
She **yelled!**
She s c r e a m e d !

She called the Witch **bad** names.

Nothing helped.
She was still locked up in the
tower.

Believe me, Rapunzel looked everywhere for a way out.

She looked behind the books; nothing there but a stone wall.

She looked under the bed; nothing there but some dust bunnies.

She lifted every rug, every piece of furniture.

There was no way out.

Every morning that voice demanded, "Rapunzel, Rapunzel, let down your hair."

Rapunzel groaned but went onto the balcony and flung her golden braid

down

down

down

to the Witch at the bottom.

The Witch grasped the braid firmly and climbed up, up, up, higher and higher until she reached the top.

"I've brought your food," the Witch would say. Sometimes she brought a favourite book or special candy. It was just like old times when they laughed over tea and the cookies that Rapunzel had baked.

But the Witch always left, and Rapunzel would be left behind in that lonely tower.

Rapunzel spent her days reading or baking. She learned to make a zillion different kinds of cookies, each one more delicious than the last.

One morning a prince was passing Rapunzel's tower on his search for a princess. His belly growled. His nose twitched. His mouth watered. Was that delicious smell cookies? Cookies in that tall, strange tower?

He got off his big, black charger and walked all the way around the tower. There was no door or even a window. So he got back on his horse and rode away.

But he kept returning. The prince was bedazzled by the smell of those cookies.

Then one day when he arrived at the tower, nose twitching and mouth watering, he heard, "Rapunzel, Rapunzel, let down your hair."

To his amazement, a golden braid flew down to the ground.

His eyes nearly popped out of his head when a Witch grabbed that braid and climbed to the top of the tower.

That night he returned and tried his luck. "Rapunzel, Rapunzel, let down your hair." Down it came.

The prince huffed and puffed on his climb. He wasn't in shape like the Witch, but finally he made it to the top.

Rapunzel invited him in for tea and cookies. He rushed in. Cookies! Time after time he returned to visit.

He grew to like Rapunzel, even love her a little. She wasn't a princess, but she made delicious cookies. She was smart and she made him laugh.

One unlucky day the Witch spied the prince as he was leaving. She waited until he mounted his horse and galloped away, then called in her sweetest voice, "Rapunzel, Rapunzel, let down your hair."

Grabbing the braid, that Witch fairly flew to the top.

"You **bad, bad** girl!" screeched the Witch. Her
teeth clicked and clacked.

From her bag she took a pair of sharp gardening
shears and cut off Rapunzel's hair.

Rapunzel floated right up to the ceiling!
Finally...Rapunzel came down.

She said to the Witch, "Well, now you've
done it. How is either one of us going
to get out of here?"

Then clever Rapunzel said, "You also have very
long hair. Let's braid it, and I will climb down
and get a big ladder and come back for you."
The Witch could see no other way.

Rapunzel braided the Witch's long
black hair. Then she climbed
all the way down to the bottom.

Rapunzel clapped her hands. "I'm free!" she said. "Free!" She stuck her tongue out at the Witch watching from the balcony.

"See how you like being locked up in there!" Then she ran as fast as her legs would carry her, far, far away from the terrible tower.

But Rapunzel wasn't the kind of girl who could leave the Witch locked up without food.

She thought and thought. Just how could she get the Witch out without getting herself back in?

"The Woodsman!" she cried. "He'll be able to climb to the top and get her out."

But when the woodsman arrived at the tower, all he found was a long, golden braid of hair hanging from the balcony.

No Witch.

The prince heard whispers that Rapunzel had escaped from the tower. He searched the countryside for her. When he found her, he begged for her hand in marriage.

Rapunzel said, "No, thank you. I'm going to start a cookie factory."

FOR SALE
COOKIES
EGGS

She did! Her cookies sell around the world. You've probably eaten some of them yourself.

The prince found his princess and is happily married with nine children.

The Witch was never heard from again.